Great big gorilla hugs for Cheryl

SIMON & SCHUSTER BOOKS FOR YOUNG READERS
An imprint of Simon & Schuster Children's Publishing Division
1230 Avenue of the Americas, New York, New York 10020
Copyright © 2005 by Derek Anderson
SIMON & SCHUSTER BOOKS FOR YOUNG READERS is a trademark of Simon & Schuster, Inc.
Book design by Mark Siegel and Jessica Sonkin
The text for this book is set in Bookman.
The illustrations for this book are rendered in acrylic paint.
Manufactured in China
2 4 6 8 10 9 7 5 3 1
Library of Congress Cataloging-in-Publication Data
Anderson, Derek, 1969-
Gladys goes out to lunch / written and illustrated by Derek Anderson.— 1st ed.
p. cm.
Summary: Gladys the gorilla is tired of eating nothing but bananas, until the day she
smells something wonderful that lures her from the zoo in search of a new treat.
ISBN 0-689-85688-1
[1. Gorilla—Fiction. 2. Foods—Fiction.] I. Title.
PZ7.A53313Gl 2005
[E]—dc22
2004016374

GLADYS
GOES OUT TO LUNCH

Written and Illustrated by
Derek Anderson

Simon & Schuster Books for Young Readers
New York   London   Toronto   Sydney

Gladys loved bananas.

She ate bananas for breakfast, bananas for lunch, and more bananas for dinner.

One day the most delicious smell came drifting through the zoo. It smelled even better than bananas. So Gladys went out for lunch.

She couldn't wait to taste what was making that
deliciously sweet scent. She followed it all the way to . . .

There were pizzas with pepperoni, pesto, and even pineapple.
Gladys tried them all. But pizza wasn't what she smelled.

When she found the sweet scent again, Gladys snooted, wiggled her toes, and followed it down the street to . . .

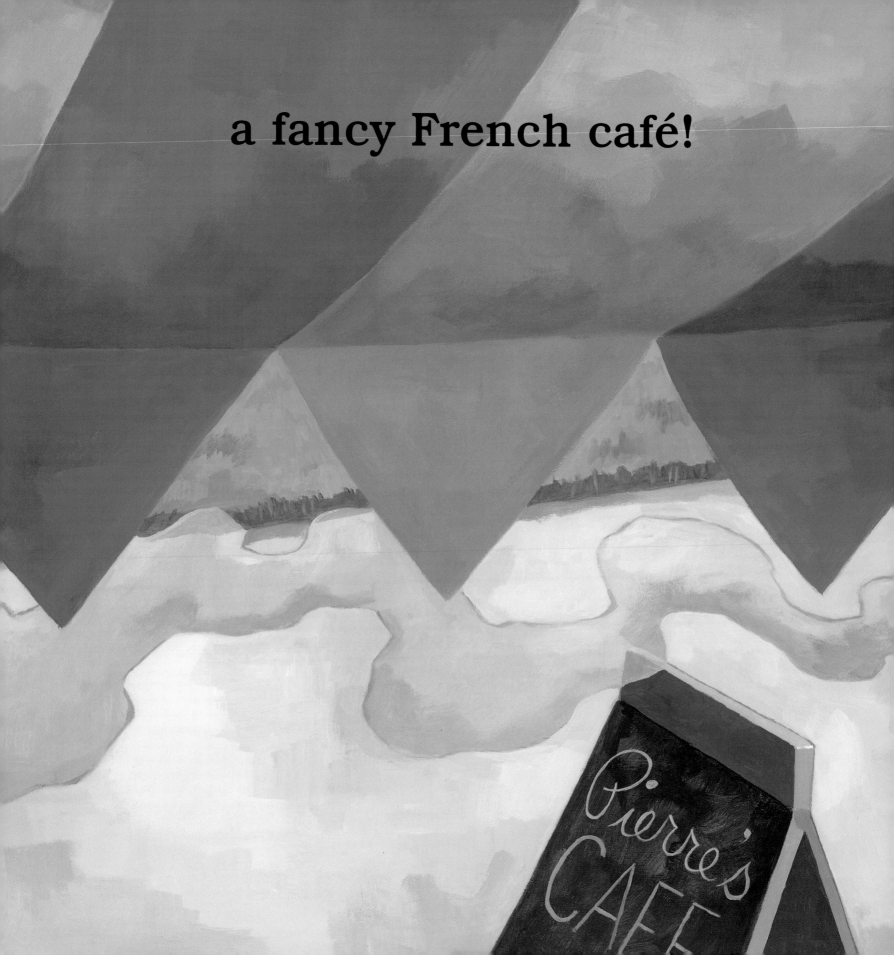

a fancy French café!

Pierre's
CAFÉ

This had to be where the smell was coming from.
There were frog legs, fried snails, and a frozen
mousse. Gladys tried them all. But fancy French
food wasn't what she smelled either. Gladys was
glad because there wasn't enough on the table
to feed a bird.

When she found the sweet scent again, Gladys snorted,
kicked up her heels, and followed it around the corner to . . .

an ice-cream stand!

Gladys hoped the smell was coming from here. There were fifteen flavors of ice cream in fifteen different colors. Gladys tried them all. But ice cream wasn't what she smelled. Gladys was tired and her tummy was nearly full.

Until she smelled that deliciously sweet scent one more time. Gladys knew she was close. She smiled, licked her lips, and followed it around the block to the back entrance of the zoo.

She sniffed all the way to a little food cart and found just what she was looking for . . .

banana bread!

Gladys ate the whole loaf by herself. It was the warmest, sweetest lunch she'd ever tasted. But there was something missing. . . .

Her favorite dessert!

Author's Note

After first writing *Gladys Goes Out to Lunch* a few years ago, I sat down one Saturday to work on a sample painting of Gladys. My wife, Cheryl, decided to inspire me by baking a loaf of banana bread. I was painting away in my studio when I heard a gasp of shock from the kitchen, so of course I went running. Cheryl was standing, wide-eyed, over an open cookbook. "Just look," she said. I looked at the recipe for banana bread and there, beneath the title, was the author's name—Gladys. I'm not now, nor have I ever been, a cook, so I'd never had a reason to open this cookbook before. I'd chosen the name "Gladys" for my gorilla only because I liked the name. And banana bread had always played a key role in the story. I don't know whether life imitates art, or art imitates life, but it seems this story was meant to be.—D. A.

BANANA BREAD

1 cup sugar
$\frac{1}{2}$ cup shortening
2 cups bananas
2 eggs
$\frac{1}{2}$ teaspoon baking soda
1 teaspoon baking powder
$\frac{1}{2}$ teaspoon salt
2 cups flour
1 cup nuts
3 tablespoons milk

Cream shortening and sugar. Add bananas and eggs.
Put baking powder, baking soda, salt, and flour
together. Mix with other ingredients. Blend well.
Pour into 2 small loaf pans or 1 large loaf pan.
Bake at 350 degrees for about 1 hour. Test
after 45 minutes by inserting a toothpick
in the center to see if it comes out clean.

—Gladys Amundson